ML Picture
HENKES
Henkes, Kevin.
Old Bear

W9-AFB-093

WITHDRAWN

KEVIN HENKES
OLD BEAR

Greenwillow Books  *An Imprint of HarperCollinsPublishers*

Old Bear. Copyright © 2008 by Kevin Henkes. All rights reserved. Printed in the United States of America. www.harpercollinschildrens.com. Watercolor paints and ink were used to prepare the full-color art. The text type is 22-point Bernhard Gothic SG-Extra Heavy. Library of Congress Cataloging-in-Publication Data. Henkes, Kevin. Old bear / by Kevin Henkes. p. cm. "Greenwillow Books." Summary: When Old Bear falls asleep for the winter, he has a dream that he is a cub again, enjoying each of the four seasons. ISBN 978-0-06-155205-2 (trade bdg.) ISBN 978-0-06-155206-9 (lib. bdg.) [1. Bears—Fiction. 2. Dreams—Fiction. 3. Seasons—Fiction. 4. Hibernation—Fiction.] I. Title. PZ7.H389Okh 2008 [E]—dc22 2007035965 First Edition 10 9 8 7 6 5 4 3 2 1

For Virginia

FOND DU LAC PUBLIC LIBRARY

By the time Old Bear
fell asleep for the winter,
it was snowing hard.

Soon he was dreaming.

He dreamed that spring had come
and he was a cub again.

The flowers were as big as trees.
He took a nap in a giant pink crocus.

Then he dreamed that it was summer.
The sun was a daisy, and the leaves were butterflies.

Part of the sky clouded over, and it rained blueberries.

Next, he dreamed of autumn.

**Everything was yellow and orange and brown,
even the birds and the fish and the water.**

After that, he dreamed that winter was back.
The world was covered in ice.

It was night, and the sky was blazing with stars of all colors.
The cold went on forever.

**Old Bear slept and dreamed,
dreamed and slept.**

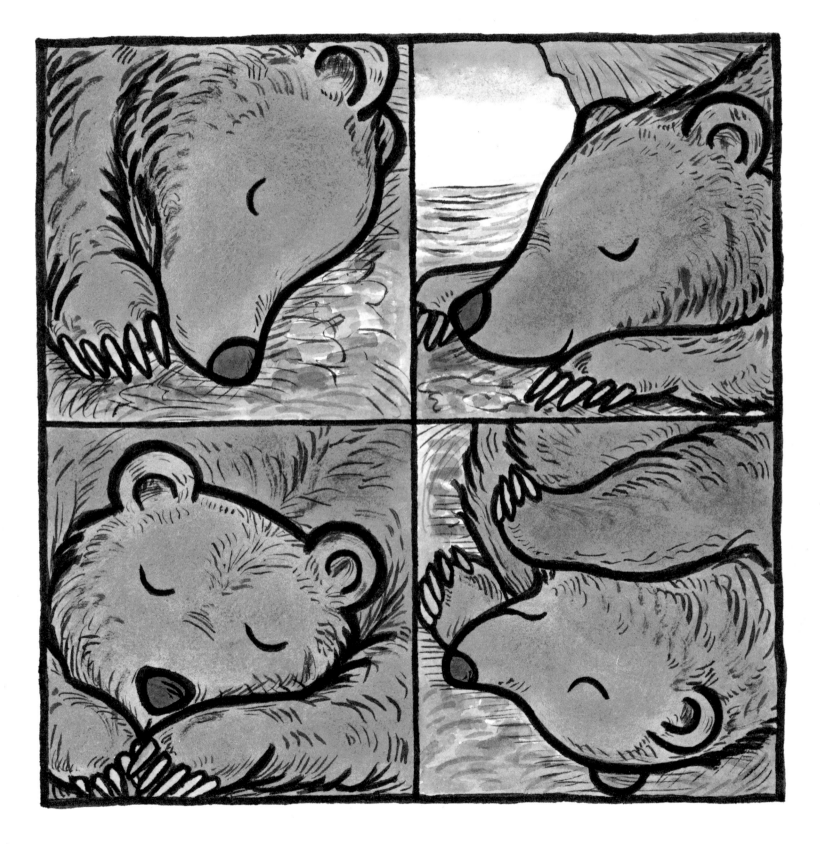

When he finally woke up,
it seemed to him that no time had passed
since he had fallen asleep.
He yawned. He stretched.

He poked his head out of his den
to see if it was still snowing.
He blinked. And blinked again.

And when Old Bear walked out into the beautiful spring day,

it took him a minute to realize
that he wasn't dreaming.